SECRET MISSION #3:
COLLISION COURSE

BY GREG FARSHTEY

SCHOLASTIC INC.

No part of this publication may be reproduced, stored in a retrieval system, or transmitted in any form or by any means, electronic, mechanical, photocopying, recording, or otherwise, without written permission of the publisher. For information regarding permission, write to Scholastic Inc., Attention: Permissions Department, 557 Broadway, New York, NY 10012.

ISBN 978-0-545-47670-6

LEGO and the LEGO logo are trademarks of the LEGO Group. © 2013 The LEGO Group. Produced by Scholastic Inc. under license from the LEGO Group.

Published by Scholastic Inc. SCHOLASTIC and associated logos are trademarks and/or registered trademarks of Scholastic Inc.

12 11 10 9 8 7 6 5 4 3 2 1   13 14 15 16 17/0

Printed in the U.S.A.   40

First printing, January 2013

Prologue

The swarm hungered.

As they flew through space, the entities that made up its mass reached out in search of that which they needed to survive. But they were unlike the ordinary creatures of this universe, for they did not seek energy or radiation or even meat to satisfy their hunger.

No, only one thing could nourish them: knowledge.

There were dozens upon dozens of them, small masses of soft organic tissue creased with furrows. Individually, they looked repulsive yet somehow fragile, but in a swarm they were something else: absolutely frightening.

They swam through the void of space, searching for intelligent life. When the creatures left their home world, they had been part of a much larger swarm. They had a mission and a purpose. But shortly after their departure, a solar storm had separated this group from the rest. Now they found themselves on the sparsely populated frontier of the galaxy, with little chance of finding what they needed to sustain them.

And then . . . one of the creatures sensed something in the cold and the dark. As soon as it did, all the others felt it, too. A source of knowledge was headed toward the swarm at high speed. If they could seize it, they would gain the strength to find and rejoin the larger swarm and resume their mission.

Nothing could be more important than the task they had been ordered to carry out. After all, it was vital to the future of the galaxy that Hero Factory be *destroyed*.

"This is the ship's log, Captain Aquax speaking," the robot said to the computer console. "The *Valiant* is three days out from space dock, on a first patrol of the frontier. Although it is the finest ship in the fleet by far, there is always the possibility of problems with a new vessel. I have instructed the crew to pay particular attention to any problems with the sensors or equipment."

Captain Aquax walked swiftly down the wide corridor of Deck 4, his metal feet clanging against the steel flooring. Now and then, a crewbot rushed past, pausing only to salute the superior officer. Everyone was a little on edge. No matter how experienced you were at space travel, the first voyage on a new ship brought out the rookie in everyone.

The *Valiant* was the culmination of years of planning and engineering work by some of the best scientists on the planet Gronnd. It was as far beyond the other ships that patrolled the frontier as a robot was beyond an ant. Powered by a tri-nuclear fusion engine and armed with mass drivers and high-intensity lasers, it was ready for almost anything, from pirates to asteroids to alien invasion.

The reason for the construction of the *Valiant* was simple: Hero Factory, as big and as successful as it was, could not be everywhere. When a crisis like the recent mass breakout of criminals occurred, the Heroes could be tied up for days or weeks trying to get things under control. That often left frontier planets on their own. Up to now, those worlds had been relying on converted ore freighters and small transports for defense, and the pirates on the outer rim of the galaxy laughed at those.

The *Valiant* was intended to change all that. It was as powerful as anything Hero Factory had, and the mere fact of its existence would hopefully be enough to scare the bad guys. If not, a few laser blasts would get the job done. If even that didn't work, the ship was carrying a quantity of highly explosive galedanium on board, enough to turn a small moon into rubble.

For now, though, Aquax just wanted to have a good first run and make it back to space dock without anything breaking down or misfiring. New designs that looked great on computer screens sometimes didn't translate well into the real world.

"Xera to Captain Aquax." The science officer's voice came over the intercom, so loud it startled Aquax. He made a mental note to have someone turn down the volume.

Hitting the comm button on the wall, he said, "Aquax here."

"Captain, we've picked up an . . . anomaly in our deep space scans. At first, I thought it was an error, so I ran a level four diagnostic on all systems. Everything checks out so far, but . . ."

"You don't sound very confident in the test results, Xera."

The science officer hesitated. "I have no reason to doubt the ship's computers' ability to scan and identify problems. But sensors are giving readings that make no sense. If there isn't something wrong with them, well, I am not sure what's out there, sir."

Aquax frowned. He had known Xera for

years, even requested him for this crew. It wasn't like him to sound so unsure.

"I'll meet you on the bridge," said Aquax. "Out."

The *Valiant*'s bridge was a hive of activity when Aquax stepped out of the elevator. Xera was standing up front, near the navigator's station, staring at the main viewscreen. Aquax wasn't sure why, since the screen seemed to be showing a normal starfield.

"What do you see?" he asked Xera.

"That's the problem," Xera replied. "I don't see anything . . . not anything out of the ordinary, anyway."

Aquax moved to join him at the screen. "All right, what is it you expect to see?"

Xera hit a button on the navigation console. The screen changed to the sensor readout. A large number of objects appeared, represented by pinpoints of light. They were still a good distance away, but based on their headings, they were on a collision course with the *Valiant*.

"Meteor shower?" suggested Aquax.

Xera shook his head. "Watch this. Computer, rewind to 001.03.457."

The screen blinked. It was now showing conditions as they had been fifteen minutes before. The mass of lights was still there, only now they were veering away from a sun.

"There was no nearby source of gravity to account for that movement," said Xera. "Those things changed course, Captain."

Now Aquax understood Xera's worries. For the objects to alter their direction required that they be intelligent, or else that they were being guided by another intelligence. Either way, it meant this was no natural phenomenon, but a potential threat.

"Battle stations!" Aquax ordered. An alarm immediately began to sound throughout the ship. "Can the sensors tell us anything about those things, Xera?"

"They're just coming into view of our

long-range scanners now, sir," Xera answered, bending over to check a readout. A moment later, he turned back to his commander with a shocked look. "Captain, according to these readings . . . they are made up of organic matter."

"Are you certain?" asked Aquax.

"I've double- and triple-checked. They are organic . . . and they're alive."

Aquax's mind sifted through possibilities. It was possible this was some flock of space creatures, obviously capable of surviving in the airless void, who were migrating and had no idea a ship was in their path. *Or not,* he thought darkly. *If they are some form of alien life, this could be the start of an attack on our galaxy.*

"Oh my . . ." Xera whispered. "Sir, I have an energy reading coming from the . . . objects."

"What kind of energy?"

"It's electrical, sir, but a very unique type," said Xera. "Captain, I think those things are . . . living brains!"

1

Breez stuck her head into the auxiliary control room. It was the twelfth place she had looked in her hunt for Rocka, and at first, it seemed this would be another failure. She was starting to get annoyed. If her teammate would just answer his communicator, she could have relayed Stormer's message and gone back to her training. But, no, Rocka had shut his comm system off—again—and she had to wander all over Hero Factory looking for him.

She was about to move on when she noticed Rocka's legs sticking out from under a console. "What are you doing down there?" she said. "Stormer has me looking everywhere for you!"

"Working," answered Rocka. "I had some ideas for how to improve our alert system and I wanted to try them out."

"And your comm?"

"It kept going off and distracting me, so I shut it off."

Breez looked down at the ground and mentally counted to ten. When she had calmed down a little, she said, "Stormer has called a meeting. You need to be there. Fix whatever you've broken and let's go."

Rocka rolled out from under the console, a smile on his face. "I haven't broken anything. I've made it better!"

"Right, come on," said Breez, turning back to the corridor. "We're late."

The rest of the team was already assembled when Breez and Rocka made it to the meeting room. Only Stringer was absent, but everyone knew he was tied up with an ongoing mission in a distant sector of the galaxy. Stormer stopped speaking when they walked in, waiting impatiently for the two to find seats before resuming.

"All right, as I was saying, things have been quiet for a while now," said the Alpha Team leader. "We've recaptured all of the major criminals who escaped in the breakout. The minor ones are being scooped up by local law. Bulk and Furno have done a good job reviewing security in our jail so that sort of thing will never happen again."

"And what if it does?" asked Evo.

"Then they're both fired," Stormer replied instantly.

Did he just make a joke? Breez said to herself. *Nah, couldn't be.*

"You all did excellent work during this recent crisis," Stormer continued. "I am sure I speak for Mr. Makuro, founder of Hero Factory, when I say that the entire galaxy owes you a debt. And that's why I am doubling everyone's training sessions, as of tomorrow."

"W-What — ?" sputtered Furno.

"Doubling?" exclaimed Rocka. "As in 'making twice as long'?"

Stormer nodded. "You all just fought some

incredible battles against some tough foes. It's only natural to want to relax a little after something like that . . . maybe let a few of your duties go, cut back on your workouts. But we're Hero Factory. We can't afford to take time off or go soft. Nor can we afford to get big heads just because we beat some villains that we had already beaten at least once before."

There was muted grumbling throughout the room, but the Heroes had to admit that Stormer was right. They had beaten Black Phantom and the other villains, but it had been close. When you worked in this job, you never knew when or where trouble was going to appear. You had to be ready.

As if to emphasize that point, the room was suddenly filled with the earsplitting wail of the danger alert. It was always loud, but now it was practically deafening. Suspecting this was one of Rocka's improvements, Breez looked at him, who just smiled and shrugged.

"Furno, patch in the alert feed," Stormer ordered. "And somebody shut off that alarm!"

Furno hit a button on the nearest console. The danger alert screen appeared at the front of the room. It was showing big trouble: a massive asteroid careening through space, apparently on a collision course with Hero Factory.

"All Heroes on full alert!" Stormer barked. "Get ships in the air now—we need to divert that rock before it hits!"

"Um, Stormer, we might want to hold off on that," said Bulk. "Take a look at the distance marker on the screen."

Stormer did as Bulk suggested. To his surprise and annoyance, the number in the lower left-hand corner of the screen showed that the asteroid was more than half a galaxy away from Hero Factory. It was no more a menace to the facility than a thunderstorm on a frontier world would be. More than likely, it would never even reach the planet Makuhero City sat on, let alone impact it.

"Cancel the alert," Stormer said, ice in his tone. "And explain to me why our sensors are picking up events on the other end of the galaxy."

Rocka raised his hand. "That would be my fault, sir."

"It would be. I see," said Stormer. "The rest of you, go back to work. Rocka, you stay here."

The other Heroes stood up and filed out of the room. Bulk paused to give Stormer a look that said, *Go easy on the kid.* Stormer responded with a slight shake of his head, which told Bulk he should stay out of this.

When Stormer and Rocka were alone, the Alpha Team leader turned to stare at the screen. "Care to explain this?"

"I . . . made some improvements. I've extended the range of the sensors by a factor of twelve, and —"

"And now we're going to be getting alerts about threats that don't exist because you adjusted the sensors without calibrating the danger scanner," Stormer finished for him.

"I was going to get around to that," Rocka finished uncomfortably.

"Listen, Rocka, you've shown yourself to be a Hero with real potential," said Stormer. "You've made some vital contributions on our missions. But since your fight with Black Phantom, you seem to be restless."

"It took me too long to catch him," Rocka replied. "He played me like an amateur before I finally brought him down."

"You were overconfident," Stormer agreed. "But we all got our bruises as a result of the breakout. You don't need to try so hard to impress your teammates. We all know what you can do."

Rocka smiled. "So does that mean I don't have to undo the work I did on the sensors?"

Stormer glanced back at the screen. "Not right now. When Stringer gets back, I want him to check them out. If he's okay with the modifications, well, we'll find some way to make it work."

"Thanks," said Rocka. "And, hey, maybe we'll spot something important before then. You never know."

"This could be incredibly important," said Xera.

"Or a sensor glitch," Aquax answered. "Disembodied brains flying through space? Sounds like something out of an old monster vid."

"It's a new species," said Xera, wonder creeping into his voice. "Something never before seen in this section of the universe. Can you imagine if we could capture one alive and study it?"

"I've got a better idea," came a voice from behind the two robots. "Why don't you remove your internal computer, toss it out an airlock, and let it swim upstream with those things?"

The voice belonged to Kirch, head of security for the *Valiant*. He hadn't been Aquax's pick for the job. He had been forced on the captain by senior officers, who wanted someone loyal only to the fleet in that important job. Kirch and Xera had been fighting since the day they met.

"I don't know what those things are, and neither do you," Kirch continued. "But you are *not* bringing one on board this vessel. Am I clear?"

"You're a security robot," Xera snapped. "I wouldn't expect you to understand the needs of science."

"And you're a scientist," Kirch replied. "I wouldn't expect you to have any common sense."

"Enough," said Aquax. "Xera, find out as much as you can about those creatures. Once we know more, we can make an informed decision on how to proceed. Kirch, I want a Level One alien presence security drill, just in case something gets on board. Dismissed."

Xera took the elevator, headed down to the labs. He was furious at Kirch. There was at least a chance he could have talked the captain into letting him bring one of the creatures aboard by tractor beam into a secure holding cell, but once the security robot spoke up, that hope was ended. Now he would be limited to studying the things via computer and sensor scan, never getting to see one close up. *What a loss to science,* he thought.

Then a thought struck him. Aquax had ordered him to find out as much as he could about the beings, hadn't he? He hadn't said anything about *how* Xera should go about doing that.

The elevator doors opened. Xera didn't get

out. Instead, he hit another button, sending the lift down to the shuttlecraft hangar bay.

Breez planted her feet and braced herself. An instant later, several panels slid aside in the wall in front of her and rocket-powered hunks of steel — called "rammers" — flew right at her. The test was simple: dodge all the flying metal for sixty seconds or get hit by one or more and wind up in the repair bay.

At first, she was able to handle the pace with ease, moving swiftly to her left or right to allow the rammers to fly by. Then the training system adjusted to her success, firing the missiles more rapidly and in a random pattern. Now Breez had to struggle to keep up. As the rate of launch got faster, it was almost inevitable she would make a mistake.

It came with fifteen seconds left on the clock. A rammer struck her a glancing blow on the right shoulder, just enough to throw her off balance. She stumbled right into the path of another projectile, this one went right for her head.

There was no time to dodge, she knew. All she could hope to do was throw herself backward at the last moment and try to ride with the impact. If she was lucky, she would just wind up severely damaged, not destroyed.

There was a sudden blast of heat. Before Breez's startled eyes, the rammer melted in mid flight into a puddle of molten metal on the floor. She turned to see Furno standing in the doorway, smoke wafting from his weapon. He hit the master control that shut down the training program.

"Stop acting like me," Furno said, reaching down to help her to her feet.

"What do you mean?" she asked. "And thank you, by the way."

"Hero Factory rules say there always has to be someone in the control room when the rammers are being used," he answered. "You were running the test alone, and you could have been killed,

Breez. That's not like you—that's like me."

"I needed a challenge," she said. "Are you going to tell Stormer?"

"Only if you keep lying to me," said Furno. "What's going on?"

Breez shrugged. "I guess. . . I'm just wondering what I'm doing here. During the breakout, I barely beat Thornraxx—a big bug, and I had to work to put him down. I feel like I haven't made a difference here in ages, and I don't know why. Maybe I'm not that good of a Hero?"

Furno understood how she felt. All the rookies on the team went through this at some point, himself included. When you were manufactured by Hero Factory, you were expected to be a Hero from day one. But they all knew not everyone measured up—some, like Von Nebula or Core Hunter, went bad, while others just washed out and wound up on Upsilon Team or even lower in the ranks. There was enormous pressure to succeed, not only for personal pride, but because if a Hero failed, innocents could get hurt.

"Hey, a Hero who never has doubts isn't much

of a Hero in my book," Furno said. "But you've already shown you're one of the best. If you weren't, you wouldn't be on Alpha Team."

"Thanks, Furno," said Breez. "Maybe I just need a new mission . . . a good win, you know? I need something more important to do than chasing Rocka all over the place."

"Go talk to Stormer," suggested Furno. "I'll bet he can help you find what you're looking for. After all, in a galaxy this big, there's always someone in trouble somewhere."

Kirch's voice crackled over the intercom. "Bridge, this is Security."

Aquax punched a button on his console. "Aquax here."

"Sir, did you authorize a shuttlecraft launch?"

"Shuttlecraft? No, of course not."

"Well, one just took off from the hangar bay, heading right for that swarm of alien creatures."

"Communications, patch me through to that

ship," Aquax ordered. When the red light flashed on his chair arm, it meant the signal had gone through. "Shuttlecraft, this is Captain Aquax. You are ordered to turn about and return to this ship. Do you read?"

"This is Xera, sir," came the reply. "I am on an intercept course with the aliens. I will transmit my readings back to the ship for analysis."

"Xera, get back here!" Aquax said. "We don't know what those things can do. They may be hostile. Return immediately, that is a direct order!"

"Sorry, sir, your communications are breaking up," Xera answered. "I cannot read you."

Kirch broke in. "Captain, request permission to send a security team out in a second shuttle to bring Xera back by force."

"Permission denied," Aquax answered. "I'm not risking more crewbots. We will pursue the shuttlecraft until we are in tractor beam range and then bring it back into the hangar."

"I assume we will be arresting Xera upon his return?"

"Let's get him back first, then worry about that," said Aquax. "Let's just get him back."

On board the shuttlecraft, Xera was closing in on the swarm. Yes, they did resemble organic brains. This was the discovery of the century. All he had to do was capture one and bring it back to the *Valiant* alive, and his place in scientific history was assured. He just hoped the appearance of his ship would not scare the creatures off.

He couldn't know that the brains feared nothing . . . or that they were waiting impatiently for his arrival. He would be the means by which they would get on board the much larger vessel, which teemed with the knowledge they craved.

It is, the brains thought as one, *almost dinnertime*.

Bulk was passing the communications center when he thought he heard something coming from behind the door. It almost sounded like a growl. He wondered if Evo's pet wolf-lizard had gotten free — again — and was feasting on the delicate wiring of the comm system. The last time that happened, it took Stringer three days to fix everything.

Cautiously, Bulk pushed the door open. But what he saw was not a wild alien animal loose in Hero Factory. Rather, it was just Breez, seated at the monitoring station.

"Um, did someone just growl at us over the radio?" asked Bulk.

"No," Breez answered.

"I see. So . . . was that you?"

"Yes."

"Mind if I ask why you're growling?"

Breez turned around to look at him. "I took Furno's advice."

"Never a good idea. Go on."

"I went and asked Stormer for a new assignment. I thought he'd give me a mission, something with a challenge to it. Instead, he sends me in here to monitor long-range communications. He says he wants to correlate what I'm picking up with what Rocka's sensor upgrade is showing."

Bulk nodded. "Not very exciting, but I can see the importance. Still . . . I'm supposed to go on a patrol in the next sector over, to watch for smugglers. I could maybe say my hydraulics are acting up and you could take my place."

Breez smiled brightly. "Would you? That would be just the best. If I don't get out of here soon, I'll go space-crazy!"

"Okay, I'll—"

Bulk's comment was cut off by a crackle of

static over the radio followed by a voice saying, "Shuttlecraft, this is Aquax. Do not, repeat, do *not* engage the creatures. Return to the ship immediately."

"That doesn't sound good," said Bulk.

"No, it doesn't," agreed Breez. Her fingers were already flying over the console, trying to get a fix on the source of the broadcast. After a few moments, she said, "Long way out, on the frontier. It's coming from a ship called the *Valiant.*"

"Keep on this," Bulk said, leaning over her shoulder to look at her scanner. "Package what you know now and get it to Stormer. It sounds like if that shuttlecraft doesn't turn back, we might be needed."

Breez nodded. But even as she sent a copy of the transmission to her team leader, she wondered — what could Hero Factory do in time? Whatever was going on out there, she feared the crew of the *Valiant* was on its own.

Success!

Xera smiled as he watched the brain squirm in the vacuum jar. With a little luck and some skill with a tractor beam, he had been able to separate one creature from the swarm, capture it, and bring it into the ship. Better yet, his actions hadn't provoked any hostile response from the others of its kind.

They had to have noticed, he thought. *Perhaps they are on a migration of some kind and can't afford to worry about stragglers. Or perhaps they are not intelligent creatures at all and only recognize threats to the swarm as a whole. I'll know more when I study this specimen.*

Satisfied with his efforts, he punched new coordinates into the navigational computer and turned the ship toward home. Kirch would want him court-martialed and Captain Aquax would be furious over his "interpretation" of orders, but Xera didn't care. He had a scientific find unmatched anywhere.

As he brought the shuttle in for a landing on

the hangar bay, he could see one of Kirch's security teams waiting for him. Xera shut down the systems and picked up the vacuum jar, holding it under his arm as he disembarked. As soon as the security robots saw it, they moved in to try and take it away from him.

"Back off!" snapped Xera, taking a step back into the ship.

"They aren't going to listen to you," said Kirch, walking into the hangar with Aquax by his side. "You're under arrest."

"I'll decide who does and does not get arrested on my ship," Aquax said.

"But, sir —"

"At ease, Kirch," Aquax said firmly. "Xera, give me one good reason not to throw you in a cell and lose the key."

Xera held up the jar with the living brain inside it. "Here's the reason, Captain. Whether those things are hostile or not, we need to know as much as we can about them. I am the only science robot on this ship with the skill to gather what we need in the short time we have."

Aquax considered his words. If the swarm was a danger, then the safety of his ship and crew might depend on what could be learned from the captured creature. Still, he couldn't allow Xera's disobedience to go unpunished.

"You're confined to your quarters and the lab until this situation is over," the captain said. "After that, I will determine if a court-martial is in order. Kirch, I want a guard on that creature for the entire time it is on this ship."

"I'll see to it personally," said the security chief.

"Fine," Aquax replied. "Escort Xera to the lab. I'll be on the bridge."

Stormer sat in his quarters in Hero Factory and replayed the transmission Breez had sent for the third time. There was no mistaking the voice in the recording. Even after all these years, he couldn't forget Aquax.

It had been back in the early days of Hero

Factory. Stormer was still a rookie—well, all the Heroes were then—and sometimes he could be too rash and impulsive. He had been making a routine delivery of medical supplies to a frontier world when his Hero craft was fired on by smugglers. Stormer succeeded in driving them off, but then chose to pursue them without calling for backup from home base.

The move turned out to be a disaster. In fact, the "retreating" smuggler ship was just leading him into an ambush. Stormer's vessel was disabled, and he was taken captive. The smugglers planned to ransom him back to Hero Factory and then sell the technology in the Hero craft to the highest bidder.

Things looked bleak. Then one of the smugglers cut Stormer's ropes and set him free. It turned out he was local law, working undercover to break the criminal ring. He introduced himself as Aquax. Together, the two managed to escape, summon help, and then lead a raid on the smugglers' base that netted the entire gang.

After it was over, Thresher, then the leader

of Alpha Team, asked Aquax about his meeting with Stormer. Aquax said that he was certain Stormer had simply allowed himself to be captured so he could get inside the criminals' hideout. Of course, Stormer told Thresher the truth, but he never forgot how Aquax tried to cover for him.

The two robots stayed friends, but time and their careers made it difficult to be in close contact. Stormer knew Aquax had been rising in the ranks, but was surprised to find his old friend was now the captain of his own ship. He remembered Aquax talking about getting the chance to deal a real blow to crime someday — it looked like he had gotten his opportunity at last.

One other thing Stormer remembered: that through that entire fight with the smugglers, Aquax had never sounded concerned or afraid. He was in complete control all the time. But the voice on the recording belonged to a robot that was deeply worried.

What could they be facing out there? Stormer wondered.

The leader of Alpha Team felt frustrated and restless. He wanted to go investigate what was happening on Aquax's ship. But his duty demanded he stay on station, monitoring events until there was a definite need to dispatch Heroes.

Of course, given how far away they are, by the time I know there's trouble it will be too late to help, he thought. *Hmmmm . . . I have an unknown situation and two Heroes who seem to have too much time on their hands. Maybe it's time for a little scouting mission.*

Stormer punched a button on his console, activating Hero Factory's public address system. "Rocka, Breez, please report to the main briefing room immediately. I have a job for you."

3

The brain seethed with frustration. The plan to use Xcra to give the swarm an opportunity to gain entrance to this source of knowledge had so far proven a failure. Here it was, trapped in a jar and unable to aid the rest of its kind. Worse, there was all this talk of "study" and "research"—too much of that and some way might be found to neutralize the swarm. That could not be allowed.

But the creature would have to be patient, it knew. Eventually, the chance would arise to escape. Then the beings in this vehicle would realize their error in allowing any member of the swarm to enter. For where there is one, will not the rest follow?

Oh, they would. They would indeed.

"How long are you going to look at that thing?"

Kirch had his hands on his hips, standing over Xera, who was peering into a hooded viewer. The scientist had been doing that for more than half an hour, pausing only occasionally to dictate a note into the laboratory audio system.

"As long as it takes," Xera replied without looking up.

It was too dangerous to open the jar to take a sample of the brain's tissue, so Xera was doing the next best thing: running a deep scan that would eventually tell him everything he needed to know about the creature's internal workings. With luck, a way might even be discovered to communicate with the brain.

"You science bots are all the same," said Kirch. "You'll study something right up to the moment that it eats you."

Xera shrugged. "It might be worth taking that risk to gain knowledge. After all, why are robots in space if not to learn?"

Kirch had heard enough. He grabbed Xera by the shoulder and spun him around. "We are out here to watch for smugglers and pirates—that's the *Valiant*'s job. And I am out here to protect this ship from anything that might threaten it . . . including you."

Xera glanced at Kirch's hand, then back at the security chief. "I know of a metal-eating virus that can reduce a robot to dust in about thirteen seconds. So I strongly suggest you move your hand."

Kirch let the scientist go. Xera brushed imaginary dust off his shoulder and pushed past his guard. "I need something from my quarters. I'm sure your security bots outside could use a walk anyway. Don't touch anything."

Then Xera was gone.

Kirch stood alone, fuming. How dare that spineless science robot talk to him like that? Xera thought possession of that disgusting brain would shield him from the consequences of his actions, but he was wrong. He was going down for what he'd done, and Kirch would be there when it happened.

His ocular sensors drifted to the brain in the jar. Kirch had no doubt this was a hostile alien presence and a potential threat to the ship. Xera was too caught up in his research, and Aquax was just too blind to see it. But Kirch knew in his core this thing was destructive.

That was when he got the idea . . . a way to solve all his problems at once.

The creature was dangerous, but Xera needed it, alive and on the ship, to continue to escape arrest. But if the brain was dead . . .

Kirch unholstered his laser. It would be quick and easy. He could claim that the brain had escaped the jar and was attacking him. He'd had no choice but to kill it. No one would dispute that besides Xera, and Xera would be in no position to argue about anything.

The security robot aimed and unleashed a blast of laser fire. Just as he did so, the brain flung itself upward in the jar. The energy bolt shattered the containment vessel but missed the creature. The brain flew at Kirch, landing on top of the robot's head.

The bonding happened in an instant. Kirch shuddered and dropped his weapon. He was dimly aware that he could no longer make his robot body move. His thoughts became fainter and fainter until they disappeared completely, to be replaced by the thoughts of the brain that now adhered to his head.

The creature absorbed Kirch's knowledge, everything he knew about the *Valiant*, its security systems, its strengths and weaknesses. It made the body bend down to retrieve the laser weapon.

The guard normally outside the door would be absent, having escorted Xera back to his quarters. The Kirch creature knew it couldn't afford to be spotted, not until it had done its job.

It left the lab, heading for the auxiliary control room. It was time to invite its brothers inside.

"Xera to Bridge! Xera to Bridge!"

Aquax hit the call button on his console. "Bridge, this is Aquax."

"The brain is gone! The jar is shattered and the brain is gone!"

Aquax leapt to his feet. "I thought Kirch was guarding it."

"He's gone, too! I think he stole the creature, Captain—he has to be stopped."

"Calm down," said Aquax. "I'm on my way."

The captain hit another button. "Security, this is Aquax. Initiate a Stage Six-Omega lockdown on all decks. There is an alien creature possibly loose on board the ship. Track down and apprehend. Also find and detain Commander Kirch. Out."

Aquax started for the elevator, only to be stopped by the navigator's voice. "Captain, the swarm has changed course and speed. They're coming right at us, sir!"

"Raise the energy shields," Aquax ordered.

The navigator hit the control button once,

twice, then turned to the captain. "Nothing, sir. Shields do not respond."

"Why not? We have plenty of power."

"Shield control has been rerouted to auxiliary control and . . . sir, someone has opened the Number Four Airlock!"

"Close it!"

More buttons were pushed, again with no result. "I can't, Captain. Everything is frozen."

Aquax stayed calm. This wasn't his first crisis. He knew the crew would take their cue from his behavior, so it was best not to let on how bad he suspected things were about to get.

"What's the heading of the creatures?"

"140.2 degrees, sir," said the navigator. "They're headed straight for the airlock."

Of course they are, thought Aquax. "Get security down to that airlock. Tell them anything that comes through it is to be considered an extreme danger to this ship and crew."

"Yes, sir."

Aquax wheeled around to another station.

"Communications, send out a distress signal. Give our position and say we are about to be boarded by an alien species."

Without waiting for a response, he got in the elevator heading for the lab. If he was right about what was happening, he was going to need Xera's help.

Stormer had just finished his briefing of Rocka and Breez. Their mission was to travel at the best possible speed to the *Valiant*, find out what was happening there, and assist if necessary. Rocka had suggested they use the personal rocket packs he had recently designed. The packs even came with upgraded shields to protect them from the extreme temperatures of space. The two would carry with them the full authority of Hero Factory, meaning even Captain Aquax would have to listen to them.

"Aquax is tough but smart," Stormer was saying. "Be honest with him and let him know what his options are, if any. He'll do the right thing."

Furno's voice suddenly broke in over the comm system. "Stormer, the *Valiant* just sent a distress call. It sounds like they're under attack."

"Pirates?" asked Stormer.

"If only," said Furno. "They're saying aliens."

"Right," said Stormer. He turned to Rocka. "You two better get going. And remember: If this looks too big for two Heroes, call for help. I am pretty sure Aquax doesn't want to make a habit of bailing out Heroes who get in over their heads."

Rocka and Breez glanced at each other, neither one knowing just what their team leader was talking about.

Minutes later, Breez and Rocka stood outside Hero Factory. The stars overheard looked inviting, but beyond them there was a mystery to be solved.

"Ready?" asked Rocka.

"Let's do it," said Breez.

Together, each equipped with a personal rocket pack, they soared off into space, heading for a danger they could not begin to imagine.

It had been three hours since the two Heroes had departed Makuhero City on their mission. There had been no word from them, but that was to be expected. Even with the extreme speed of the rocket packs, they would still be some distance from the *Valiant*.

There had been no further distress calls or, indeed, any radio traffic at all from the ship. So far as the sensors could tell, no other vessels had come to the *Valiant*'s aid. But there had been signs of alien life in the vicinity, life-forms that mysteriously disappeared off the screens, never to reappear.

Stormer was satisfied that Hero Factory would

be first on the scene to offer help and assistance. Local law meant well, but they didn't have the training that Alpha Team members had. Locals tended to learn as they went, while a Hero spent his or her entire existence preparing for their job.

Although they didn't have the experience of Bulk or Stringer, Rocka and Breez should have been able to handle whatever they encountered. Part of being a Hero was anticipating every possible situation and preparing a plan to deal with it. Those few moments of paralysis following a shocking surprise could be fatal in this line of work. A Hero was trained not to freeze up, but to act.

Furno's voice broke into his thoughts via the com-link. "Stormer, I think you better get up here. Either Rocka's sensors are way out of order or something really weird is happening on that ship."

When Stormer reached the control center, he saw that Furno had the sensor readout up on the main screen. At first, the Alpha Team leader didn't see the problem. Then his keen optics noted the incredible speed at which the *Valiant* was now traveling.

"How long?" he asked Furno.

"Just now," the fiery Hero replied. "The ship suddenly changed course and took off. At the rate they're traveling, they'll either cross the galaxy in record time or blow themselves to atoms. But that's not the worst part. Look at this."

The screen switched to a view of the entire galaxy. A flashing red line indicated the projected course of the *Valiant*, as determined by the Hero Factory computer system.

The ship was headed straight for the Maku-hero Asteroid Belt. The computer's best estimate had it on a collision course with Hero Factory. "The ship's manifest has it listed as carrying galedanium," said Furno. "If it hits, the resulting explosion will destroy the factory, the city, and just about everything else for a light-year all around."

"Confidence level?" Stormer asked. It was a quick way of asking Furno how certain he felt about the computer's findings.

"They are still far enough away that they could change course," Furno conceded. "But . . . first they say aliens are attacking, and then the ship is suddenly rocketing right for Hero Factory—the first line of defense against an invasion. I think we're being targeted, Stormer."

Bulk had walked in while Furno was talking. A low whistle escaped his mouth. "I knew we shouldn't have given out our address," he joked.

"Options, Bulk," said Stormer. The team leader would already have possible courses of action in his head, but he relied upon the advice of his veterans as well.

"Sit here and hope they don't hit us, or make sure they don't," Bulk answered. "We can probably scrape up enough firepower to knock them out of the sky."

Stormer shook his head. "We have to factor in the possibility that the ship has been hijacked. That means there are innocent robots on board. We can't just blow them up."

"Stormer," Bulk said, his voice low, "if that ship hits us, all those robots will be dead anyway . . . along with a whole lot of other innocents."

"Didn't you say something about knowing the captain of that ship?" asked Furno.

"Yes," Stormer replied. "I've known him a long time."

"Is he the type who would let someone steal his ship?"

"No. No, he's not."

"Then I have to agree with Stringer," said Furno. "If the aliens, whatever they are, managed to take the ship from your friend, they have to be considered extremely dangerous. Who's to say what they might do next if they succeed in destroying Hero Factory?"

Stormer started for the door. "So it's two to one in favor of blowing up the *Valiant*," he said. "Too bad Hero Factory isn't a democracy."

Rocka and Breez were racing through space when the broadcast from Hero Factory finally reached them. It was Furno, saying, "Rocka, Breez, condition red, repeat, condition red. The *Valiant* is now assumed to be under hostile control."

"Wonderful," said Rocka. "So we can expect to be fired on, then."

"The ship is on a 234.5-degree heading, approaching maximum sublight speed and getting faster every second. Intercept with caution and report what you find. We will keep this channel open. Hero Factory out."

"Maximum sublight?" said Breez. "Can these rocket packs go that fast?"

"If they have to," Rocka answered. "The question is: Can our bodies move that fast? If we pass the stress point of our robot forms, they'll be ripped apart by our speed."

"And if they're not?" asked Breez.

"Then we get to find a way to stop a runaway spaceship," smiled Rocka. "Well, we wanted some adventure in our lives. Looks like we got it."

Bulk was on his way to his quarters when he saw Stormer emerging from the armory. The Alpha Team leader was wearing one of Rocka's rocket packs.

"Going somewhere?" asked Bulk.

"I'm going after Rocka and Breez," Stormer replied, without breaking stride. "You're in charge until I get back. Tell Furno to keep trying to get in contact with Stringer. He's been radio silent for too long."

"Wait a minute," said Bulk, turning to follow his commander. "You assigned those two to do the job. Why don't you let them do it?"

"Because it might be too big," Stormer answered.

"Don't give me that," growled Bulk. "You're worried about your friend. Why not just admit it?"

Stormer glanced back over his shoulder. "I don't make team decisions based on personal feelings."

"This isn't a team decision," Bulk countered. "This is Stormer wanting to make sure an old pal is okay. You're allowed to have feelings, you know."

Stormer ignored him. "If the *Valiant* stays on its current course and enters any adjacent solar system, I want you to scramble every available Hero craft and bring that ship down. Clear?"

"What about the three of you?"

"Bulk, if we haven't been able to stop that ship by the time it gets here, you won't need to worry about us anymore."

Rocka and Breez spotted the ship as it flashed through space. Even at high speed, Rocka noted that the ship's shields were down. That was good news. If they had been active, there would be no way he and Breez could ever get aboard.

"What's your plan?" asked Breez. "Or don't you have one?"

"We intercept, find an open airlock, and get in," Rocka answered.

"What if there isn't an open airlock?"

"Then we make one," said Rocka.

The two rocketed off on a course that would

bring them close to the ship. Despite Rocka's casual attitude, Breez could tell that he was completely focused. Doing what he suggested would require split-second timing. If they missed, either the ship would leave them far behind, or worse, smash them to pieces.

There was another problem, too. If they did break into the ship, they would certainly set off alarms. Any hostile force inside would come running.

They went faster, Breez taking care to match every one of Rocka's maneuvers. She could feel the strain as the incredible speed at which they were traveling threatened to shatter her metal body.

The world around her became a blur. Dimly, she could perceive Rocka signaling her to fly toward an airlock on the port side. She forced herself to move, even though every change of direction now was incredibly risky.

Rocka had already reached the side of the ship and was pushing the rocket pack to its utmost just to keep pace. From his equipment port he produced a small laser torch. With enormous effort, he used the torch to cut through the airlock.

Now came the even more dangerous part. As the airlock was breached, Rocka had to grab on and somehow pull himself inside. Breez was right behind, wondering if she would survive this ordeal long enough to follow him in. She saw him disappear within, and then she saw something else . . . something horrifying.

The *Valiant* was equipped with all the latest technology. This included a self-sealing hull. The hole Rocka had made was already closing. Only by putting on even more speed was she going to make it.

It took everything the rocket pack had, and more than Breez thought she could muster, to get into the ship. As the metal healed behind her, she found that her left arm had been damaged by that last effort. Though still in place, it would be useless to her until she could get to a repair bay.

Rocka wasn't wasting any time. He was already hard at work trying to decipher the code to unlock the next airlock. As Breez had expected, alarms were going off. The bridge console would have recorded what they had just done as a hull breach, so a damage control team was sure to come check it out.

She scanned her weaponry. In a case like this, a Hero had to be very careful not to harm innocents by accident. At the same time, this was a case of infiltration at least and outright hijacking at worst. It made no sense under the circumstances to assume anyone was "innocent."

Rocka finally hit the right sequence of numbers, and the next airlock opened. There was one more to get through before they would be in the ship. Breez increased the range and sensitivity of her audio receptors, but heard nothing beyond the last door. Even the alarm had been shut off.

"That's weird," she said quietly.

"What?"

"Why isn't anyone rushing to investigate a hole appearing in the hull?"

"Maybe because the metal fixes itself?" suggested Rocka, as he punched in various combinations into the keypad.

Breez shook her head. "Even with that, you would still lose atmosphere with a hull breach, not to mention the possible structural damage. You can't just ignore that."

"Don't knock it. Ah, there we go," said Rocka as the door slid aside. "If we can move around the ship without being spotted, we might learn a thing or two."

Rocka crouched down, looked both ways, and then slipped into the corridor. Breez followed, but she couldn't get the nagging feeling out of her mind that something on this ship just *felt* wrong. They were on a middle deck, but there was no sign of any crewbots, not even maintenance.

Where is everyone? she wondered. *Were they injured in an attack? Did they all evacuate the ship? Or worse . . .*

Breez suppressed a shudder.

What if they're still here . . . just waiting . . . waiting for us to walk right into an ambush?

Suddenly, being stuck behind a communications console did not seem so bad.

5

tormer checked his wrist chronometer. He was hours behind Rocka and Breez, though going as fast as possible to try to make up the time. There had still been no word from either one of them—even if they made it to the ship, they might be worried that any broadcast would be monitored.

That kind of caution made sense. What Stormer was about to do made none. But something told him it was the right move to make.

"Preston Stormer to *Valiant*, come in, please," he said into his helmet mike.

The only answer was static.

He tried again. "This is Alpha Team Leader

Stormer of Hero Factory, requesting a Priority 1-A communication with the *Valiant*. Over."

That got an answer. Mentioning Hero Factory usually did open doors. "*Valiant* here. Proceed."

"I want to speak with Captain Aquax."

"Aquax here." It was indeed the voice of Stormer's old friend.

"Captain, what is the current status of your ship?"

There was a pause. Then Aquax responded, "All is well here, Stormer. Why do you ask?"

Stormer decided it might be best not to let the *Valiant* know they were being monitored by Hero Factory. Instead, he said, "A mining outpost reported you were heading out of your sector at a high rate of speed. Is there trouble, and if so, do you require Hero Factory's assistance?"

This time, the pause lasted longer. "Negative, Hero Factory. No aid is required. This is the first voyage of the ship, and we are having some . . . engine trouble. Our engineering team has assured us the problem will be corrected shortly."

"Sounds a lot like the problem we had with

that runaway ore freighter that time," said Stormer. "Almost wound up in a sun."

Aquax chuckled. "Right. Well . . . you can save your Heroes for robots who are really in trouble. I . . . assume you have not dispatched anyone to our ship?"

It's him, but . . . not, Stormer thought. *He responded too quickly to my last comment. It wasn't an ore freighter we were on, it was a transport ship, and we were heading for a collision with an asteroid. Aquax wouldn't forget details like that. So either someone is posing as him, or else he purposely fouled up his answer to send me a message that something's wrong.*

"No, no," Stormer lied. "I don't have Heroes to spare to send out for every broken ship. But if you don't find a way to put the brakes on, we're going to start getting calls and we may have to do something."

"Understood. Aquax out."

Stormer heard the sharp snap of the connection being broken. Now he knew he was right to send Rocka and Breez, as well as to follow himself. He also knew that all three of them were heading for serious trouble.

He squeezed the last bit of power out of his rocket pack. If his two Heroes had made it onto that ship, it might already be too late.

Aquax turned back to the bridge. "He knows."

Kirch looked at him, an expression of doubt on his face. The emotion did not belong to him, but rather to the brain creature that sat atop his head. Through his metal mouth, it said, "That's impossible."

The brain that controlled Aquax caused the captain to wave his hand, dismissively. "You have always taken Hero Factory too lightly. They have not survived — *Stormer* has not survived — this long by being slow or reckless."

"Meaning?"

"Meaning they know we are coming," said the creature controlling Aquax. "They are going to try to stop us."

Kirch turned to the navigation station, now manned by a brain-controlled crewbot. "Do sensors show any Hero craft approaching?"

"No" was the reply.

"They have nothing that can match this ship," Kirch said. "Any Heroes they send will simply meet their end a little earlier than the rest."

Aquax did not look convinced. "They will muster defenses in Makuhero City."

"We will be upon them too fast for it to do any good," Kirch replied.

The dismay of the creature linked to Aquax showed in the frown on the captain's face. "The hull breach—we have been boarded. We must send some of our host bodies to that section to stop any Heroes on this ship."

Kirch shook his head. The effect, with the brain creature affixed to the top of his head, was comical in a disgusting sort of way. "Our sensors will find them. But if you confront them too soon, they will go back the way they came and report to their superiors. Let them penetrate farther into the ship and trap themselves. Then we will make them just like us, and gain all their knowledge of Hero Factory."

No one could argue that it wasn't a sensible plan. If anything had been left of the personalities of the crew, they would have been frightened for the Heroes on board. But the brains were in control, so everyone just went back to their jobs and didn't give a second thought to what was about to happen.

"What do you think is going to happen?" asked Breez.

She was talking to Rocka, who was slapping the side of his portable sensor unit with his hand, trying to get it to work. This tactic was failing miserably.

"I don't understand," he said. "I checked all my equipment before we left Hero Factory. This was working fine."

"Maybe it still is," Breez said. "If this ship has been captured, the enemy could be jamming sensors." She smiled. "But I'll bet they're not jamming their own. Come on."

Breez and Rocka moved down the wide, empty corridor and ducked into the first open compartment. As Breez expected, there was a computer console in there, standard equipment on a ship like this.

"Keep watch," she said to Rocka.

"But shouldn't I—"

"You're not the only one who knows their way around a piece of technology," Breez gently scolded. "And I didn't come on this mission to just watch you do things."

Rocka did as he was told. Behind him, Breez used her skills to break into the *Valiant*'s computer system. What she found was puzzling and disturbing.

"Okay, I have good news, bad news, and weird news," she announced. "Where do you want me to start?"

"Wherever you like."

"We're on Deck Eight, halfway between

engineering and the command center, the two places we need to go," said Breez.

"I'm guessing that's the good news."

"You got it. The ship's internal sensors are picking up robot energies, mostly around those two spots. But I'm also seeing some other form of life . . . something organic."

"Organic?" said Rocka. "Gross."

"That's where it starts getting weird," Breez continued. "There's more of the organic life than there are active robots . . . and there aren't anywhere near enough active robots to run a ship this size."

"So the question is: Where is everyone? Did they somehow evacuate, or . . ."

There was no reason to finish the sentence. They both knew it was possible the crew had gone down fighting.

"All right," Rocka said. "We split up. You head for the bridge and see if you can find out what's going on here. I'll go to engineering and try to stop the ship. If you get in trouble, give a yell into your helmet mike and I'll come running."

Breez gestured toward the computer screen. "I've found a schematic of the ship. Better memorize it so you don't get lost."

Rocka laughed. "Breez, I can smell an engineering section five miles away. Be quick. Be careful."

"You, too," said Breez.

With that, Rocka went down the corridor and disappeared from sight. Breez didn't follow. Instead, she turned back to the ship plans on the computer screen.

There was no easy way to reach the command center. No matter what approach she took, she would have to be out in the open at some point, and a perfect target for any hostile force. No, there was only one "safe" way to get where she was going.

She hit another button and zoomed in on the map. There they were: ventilation shafts, running the length of the entire ship. It would be a tight squeeze, but she was pretty sure she could move through them. Not only would they lead her all the way up to the bridge, but she would have a vantage point from which she could observe the action and remain unseen.

Access to the shafts was through grates located all over the ship. There was one in the room she was in, located high upon the far wall. Breez shut down the computer, mounted her twin-bladed weapon and shield on her back, and walked across the room. She reached up to pull the grate loose.

A massive surge of electricity shot from the grate into her metal body, sending her hurtling across the room. She slammed into the wall and hit the floor, unconscious.

Furno walked into the Hero Factory control center. Bulk was there, keeping an eye on the galaxy map.

"Anything?" asked Furno.

"No change, kid," Bulk answered. "It's still coming at us like a comet."

"How long do we have?"

"Not long enough," answered Bulk. "The word just came down from upstairs: All non-essential personnel are being evacuated. Evo is keeping an eye on things, making sure everybody stays calm. Me, I'm not sure anyone is going to be able to get far enough away in time for it to matter."

"There has to be something we can do!" said Furno, slamming his metal fist against a console and leaving a dent.

"There is," said Bulk, striding to a communications station. He hit a button and his voice boomed over the loudspeaker system. "This is acting Alpha Team Leader Bulk. Ready all Hero craft and get them into space. Intercept and destroy the *Valiant*."

"Wait a minute!" Furno exclaimed. "Didn't Stormer say we had to wait until it got closer?"

"Yeah, he did, but I just spotted something on the screen. Take a look."

Furno glanced at the sensor screen. An object had moved into the *Valiant*'s path. Readings indicated it was an unmanned freighter, of the type common in frontier space lanes. Grimly, the two Heroes watched as the point of light that represented the *Valiant* collided with the one that stood for the freighter. A split second later, the freighter's light was gone.

"You know what that means," said Bulk. "It just rammed that freighter and destroyed it. If there had been robots on it, they would all be so much space junk now. And it's going to do the same thing to anything that tries to get in its way."

"But Breez, Rocka, and Stormer . . . you'll be condemning them to die, too, if they're on that ship."

"I know," said Bulk, looking down at the floor. "Believe me, kid, I know. But we can't be sure any of them have successfully boarded, and even if they have . . . if we wait too long, we'll only get one shot. Fail, and you can kiss off this star system. I can't take that chance, not even for three Heroes . . . three friends."

Furno heard the familiar rumble that meant Hero craft were launching. To his audio receptors, it sounded like a funeral march.

Bulk turned to go. "Where are you heading?" asked Furno. "How can you leave at a time like this?"

"I'm going to my quarters," answered Bulk, without turning around. "I'm going to write my resignation. As soon as this crisis is over, I'm quitting Hero Factory. I can't do it anymore, not with the lives of three good robots on my conscience."

Before Furno could say anything more, Bulk was gone.

6

Rocka had been on spaceships before, though never one quite this big. He didn't like them, and he especially didn't like the *Valiant*. It was too large, too new, too antiseptic. Its halls felt like they had never heard the sound of a robot's voice.

Yes, he was something of a wizard with high tech, but Rocka had a sense of history, too. He respected the inventors who had come before, the ones who had made great breakthroughs with far less to work with than he had. Maybe that was part of the reason a brand-new vessel like this one rubbed him the wrong way: It had no history.

And it's never going to have one if you don't get moving, he reminded himself.

He had figured out a relatively safe path to engineering, but it was going to take a long while to get there. Then he remembered something that brought him up short. There had to be an auxiliary control room somewhere around here—it was usually around the midlevel of a ship like this. If he could find it, he could reroute the ship's controls through there and bring the *Valiant* to a screeching halt.

It took a while to find it. Even though there was no sign of any life, robot or otherwise, on this deck, he had to proceed like enemies might be near. Not doing so might mean getting struck down and leaving Breez on her own against a ship full of invaders.

Not that she couldn't handle it, he thought, smiling. *But she probably wouldn't speak to me again.*

He spotted the auxiliary control room down a right branch off the main corridor. There was no guard outside. Rocka was pleased with that, but he also knew it was strange. A sensitive area like this would usually have security posted around it.

Even odder, the electronic lock on the door had been disabled. That made no sense. Anyone could just wander in and take over the ship.

Pretty sloppy way to run things, Rocka thought, drawing his sword and going inside.

The first thing he noticed was that there was no one on duty inside. The second thing was that it was cold in the room, really cold. He did a fast check of the climate controls. Someone had shut them down in various parts of the ship, meaning the temperature would be plunging well below freezing in those areas. Soon it would be so cold that robot bodies wouldn't function properly, at least not without some modifications.

Now I wish Furno were here, he said to himself. *He could warm things up a little.*

Rocka sat down at the console and started trying to make sense of the controls. He had two jobs to do, and they had to be done at almost the exact same time. Control of the ship had to be transferred to this chamber, and then the bridge had to be locked out from taking it back. Of course, once he did this, whoever was running the ship was going to be racing down to auxiliary control to pound on him. But he would worry about that when it happened.

The Hero got to work. So engrossed was he in his labors that he never bothered to look up.

For the room was not as empty as it had first appeared . . . a dozen brains were affixed to the ceiling, resting after their long journey through space. Now they were awakening, and realizing with satisfaction that a new source of knowledge had come to them. All they had to was have one of their number drop on Rocka, and whatever he knew would belong to them . . . and so would his body.

A brain perched above the console pulled its tiny insectoid legs free of the metal ceiling and began to fall.

Breez's vision system abruptly came back online. The sight that greeted her was an unfamiliar robot bent over her body. She sat up quickly and reached for her weapon.

"No, no, please!" the robot whispered. "I'm here to help."

"Who are you?" demanded Breez. "What's going on around here?"

"My name is Xera. I am . . . I was . . . the chief science officer for this ship. Now I'm a fugitive. But who are you? You're not part of the crew."

"I'm from Hero Factory," said Breez, getting up. She was still a little shaky from that electric jolt, but she wasn't going to let this stranger see that. "Your ship is a runaway. I'm here to stop it before it causes a disaster."

Xera laughed, but there was more sadness than happiness in the sound. "If only we were just a runaway . . . Do you think what's happening is an accident?"

He gripped Breez by the shoulders. When he spoke, Breez wasn't sure if she heard fear or madness in his voice. "We are headed toward Hero Factory to destroy it! They know you are the only force in the galaxy that can stop them. That's why you have to be wiped out, down to the last Hero."

"Wait a minute, who's 'they'? Who are you talking about?"

"The brains," Xera whispered.

"Did you say 'brains'?"

"I brought one on board. I didn't know what it was. But it got loose." Xera was talking more to himself than to Breez now. "It took over Kirch. He opened the airlock and let the rest on board. Then they . . . they took over the crew. I managed to escape and hide, but when they want to, they'll find me. After all, where can I go? We're on a spaceship."

Brains? Breez immediately thought of a recent mission in which Heroes had encountered crawling brains whose origin was unknown. So that was the organic life she had detected on the sensors. Once on board the *Valiant*, the brains had aimed the ship like a plasma blaster right at Hero Factory.

Assuming, of course, this Xera is telling the truth, she thought, *and he's not just crazy. Right now, that's a big assumption.*

"I need to reach the bridge," said Breez. "But that grate is electrified. Is there another way into the ventilation shafts?"

"The bridge?" Xera said, shocked. "But . . . they are there! They'll make you one of them!"

"I have to take that chance. Lives depend on it. Can you get me into the system?"

Xera nodded. "There's a security override code. It shuts down every security system on the ship—locks, alarms, computer firewalls—for five seconds. You won't have much time, but . . ."

"It's long enough. Do it. And . . . thanks."

Xera walked over to the computer console. He waved for Breez to stand by the grate. "Once I punch in the code, you have to move fast!"

"I'll make it to the bridge and stop this, somehow. Then I'll come back for you. Where will you be?"

Xera looked at her and shrugged. "Hiding." He tapped a nine-digit code into the computer. "Now! Go!"

Breez tore the grate off the wall and vaulted into the ventilator shaft. Xera watched her go, hoping he had done the right thing. If not, everything was surely lost.

In auxiliary control, two things happened almost simultaneously. The password-protected firewall that Rocka had been trying to hack through suddenly disappeared, thanks to the temporary shutdown of the security codes. The Hero was so excited, he jumped up out of his chair and yelled, "Yes!". . . just as a brain landed right where he had been sitting.

Rocka heard the soft sound, whirled, and let out a strangled cry of disgust. He whacked the creature with the flat of his sword, sending it flying off the chair and skittering across the room.

Where did this thing come from? Rocka wondered, glancing upward.

That was when he saw a sight that made one brain on a chair seem warm and fuzzy. All around, the brains were releasing their hold on the metal and starting to drop.

Rocka dove for the door. He hit the hallway, rolled, and sprang up to his feet just as the creatures began to crawl after him. He powered up his sword and struck the metal floor of the hallway. The energy flew through the floor and jolted the brains. The first wave of creatures was stunned, but the second just sprang off the floor and clung to the walls like spiders.

They don't need a Hero in this place, Rocka thought. *They need an exterminator.*

Every instinct told Rocka to stay and fight and crush these little monsters. But the important thing, he reminded himself, was the ship — if he wasted time here, it might be too late to stop it. It killed him to do it, but he turned and ran.

Of course, I may just be running into more of these things in engineering . . . but maybe this time I can surprise them.

"Where are they now?" asked the Kirch creature.

The navigator looked down at the sensor array. "One is on the move, heading down — possibly for the engineering deck. The other . . . no sign, sir."

Kirch nodded. The second Hero had to be in the ventilation shafts, one of the few places the internal sensors couldn't penetrate. That was regrettable . . . for the Hero.

"Sir, I'm getting something on long-range sensors," reported the navigator.

"What is it?" asked Aquax. When Kirch shot him a look, Aquax said, "This body belongs to the commander of this ship. Therefore, I — "

"But this brain belongs to the leader of our portion of the swarm," Kirch reminded him, his robot arm pointing to the creature atop his head. "So I will ask the questions on this bridge."

The navigator's answer cut off the argument. "It's very small . . . moving extremely fast . . . sir, I'm getting a life sign!"

"Onscreen!" barked Kirch. "Full magnification."

The image on the main screen changed to a

starfield off the port side. No ship or other object was visible.

"It's too small," explained the navigator . . . or, rather, the brain explained through his mouth. "The optics of these robots are not sophisticated enough to see it. But it's there."

"It's Stormer," said Aquax.

"How would you know?" asked Kirch, annoyed.

"This body knows," Aquax replied. "Stormer would never send his Heroes to do anything he wouldn't do. I told you, they know we are coming and they are responding."

"Then we will respond as well," said Kirch. "Lock on that target and fire all weapons."

"Yes, sir."

The ship shuddered as lasers and mass drivers mounted in the bow. They quickly unleashed their immense power, all at one robot-sized target.

Evo sat at the controls of his Hero craft, trying not to think about where he was heading or what he was about to do.

Bulk's orders were clear. Find the *Valiant*, destroy the *Valiant*, no matter what — even if it meant ending the lives of three Heroes.

Evo's first reaction to the orders was disbelief. How could anyone do this? And how could Hero Factory hope to survive this, once the story got out?

For a split second, Evo considered turning back. His hand hovered over the button that would reverse his course. But in his core he knew that wasn't an option. His duty was to the living beings of this star system, all of whom would be wiped out if the *Valiant* struck Hero Factory.

Stormer would understand, he thought. *And Rocka, Breez . . . I'm sorry. I'm only doing what has to be done.*

His hand shifted, his finger stabbing down on the button that triggered the thrusters. Behind him, a dozen Hero craft accelerated as well, toward a final meeting with the *Valiant*.

7

Stormer could count the moments left in his existence on one hand.

The full power of a spaceship had been turned on him. Laser fire blanketed the starfield, while mass driver pellets shot past him all around. He dodged and weaved, taking advantage of the maneuverability his rocket pack gave him. But it was only a matter of time — no robot could hope to evade computer-controlled weaponry for long.

Unless I get a little help, he said to himself.

His onboard sensors had picked up a flock of meteoroids not far away. Fragments of asteroids, these space rocks usually had a high metal content. In this particular region of space, the metal in most meteoroids caused havoc with electronic signals. Already, Stormer's sensors were being disrupted.

Without its electronic "eyes," the *Valiant* would be blind and deaf. All he had to do was find a way to make the meteoroids work for him.

Then Stormer got an idea. It would take a lot of power, but it might work. Triggering the controls of his armor, he sent powerful magnetic waves out into space. The magnetism attracted the metal in the meteoroids, drawing them toward him.

Now came the tricky part. The rocks were traveling at about twenty miles per second. If he didn't time things just right, they would batter him to pieces.

As the meteoroids approached, Stormer watched for an opening. He spotted it quickly, a gap between two large rocks. Darting forward, he simultaneously shut down the magnetic field and slipped into the middle of the group of meteoroids.

Free from the magnetic pull, the meteoroids drifted to a new course, this one putting them in line with the *Valiant*. Inside, Stormer clung to one of the fragments of rock, riding along and hoping they would get him close to the ship.

In the meantime, he could imagine the reaction on the bridge of the *Valiant*. . . .

"The target has disappeared," the navigator reported.

"Good," said the Kirch creature. "Then he has been blown to atoms."

"No, no," said Aquax. "Look again."

Kirch glanced at the screen. He didn't see anything unusual, other than some rocks drifting into the path of the ship. They would pose no problem. The *Valiant* would smash them to dust.

"What exactly are you picking up on sensors?" asked Aquax. The creature on top of his head was growing increasingly frustrated with the Kirch creature, and it showed in the tone of its host's voice.

"The readings are garbled," said the navigator. His creature was confused, wondering if it was somehow misinterpreting the readings of these alien controls.

"The metal in the asteroids is interfering with your readings," said Aquax. "So maybe Stormer is gone . . . or maybe he is still out there, and we just can't see him."

"Fine," snapped Kirch. "Blast the asteroids to powder. That should answer any questions that remain."

Breez had been crawling through the ventilation shafts for what felt like hours. They seemed to go on for miles, and she knew there was still a long way to go before she reached the bridge.

She still had no idea just what to do when she got there. A normal bridge would have ten to twelve crewbots on it at any one time, and if Xera was telling the truth, they would all be under the control of the alien brains.

Maybe I could burst in, fight my way to the navigation controls, put them on a new course, and then lock them up before they strike me down, she thought. *Right, and then Mr. Makuro will change the name to "Breez Factory." I have about as much chance of that happening as of that plan working.*

Breez paused. She'd heard something—or thought she had.

Skritch skritch skritch.

There it was again. The sound was coming from up ahead. Whatever was making that noise, she was fairly certain she didn't want to meet it. Not that there was any chance of turning back—the shafts were a decent width, but nowhere near roomy enough for her to do a U-turn. That left crawling backward, which would delay a fight by maybe three seconds.

Skritch skritch skritch.

That did it. With some effort, she unlimbered her twin-bladed lance. Maybe a few sharp pokes would get whatever was out there to back off.

She rounded a corner and saw something moving up ahead. Breez stopped. When the other occupant of the shaft was close enough to see, she gasped.

It was a brain with insectoid legs. Xera hadn't been lying. And here she was, in an airshaft, face-to-frontal-lobe with one of the monsters.

"All right," she said. "I guess this is the part where you try to take me over and I use my lance to make a cutting argument against it."

The brain stopped crawling. It looked at her with its red eyes. She got the feeling it understood.

"What are you? What do you want here?" Breez asked.

The brain gave no answer.

"Won't talk — or can't talk?" said Breez. "Can you only communicate when you take someone over?"

The brain still said nothing, but it took a few tentative steps forward.

Breez resisted the urge to back away. Somehow, she knew that the second she did, this thing would spring onto her.

If she wasn't going to retreat, she had to attack. But there was no guarantee a hand-to-leg fight in a narrow space was going to go her way. But the little bit of light Breez spotted not too far down the shaft gave her an idea.

"Back up!" she snapped, prodding at the creature with her lance. "Give me some room!"

The brain moved a few steps back. She repeated the action, driving it farther down the shaft. A few times, it moved to spring, but she managed to block the attempts. The last time, it actually faked moving to the left then tried to leap at her from the right. She barely moved her lance in time to keep the creature away from her.

They had reached the site of another grate. Breez moved forward so that her head was parallel with it. The brain made something that sounded like a hiss of anger. It was now or never.

Abruptly, Breez flipped over onto the right side as if she were going to try to slip by the creature. It sprang instantly, intending to seize control of her.

In that fraction of a second, Breez pushed

herself back as hard and as fast as she could. The brain missed her, slamming into the grate. There was a flash of electricity and the creature flew backward, smashing into the opposite wall of the shaft. It fell forward then, unconscious, smoke rising from its form.

Breez started crawling past it. There was an impossibly narrow gap between its body and the grate. She would almost rather be jolted again than have to touch that thing.

Rocka had made it to the engineering deck. Two guards were standing by a pillar at the entrance to the main engineering center. Both of them had those brain creatures sitting on top of their heads.

Well, that's certainly disgusting, thought Rocka. *I'm not sure there's enough metal cleaner on Hero Factory to wipe these images out of my mind.*

They hadn't spotted him yet. Rocka hurled his shield at the pillar, mentally triggering the whirling blades on the edges of the disc. It struck the pillar, neatly slicing through the metal. When the guards turned to look at the damage, Rocka ran toward them. Using his sword like a vaulting pole, he flew feetfirst at the guards and slammed them into a wall. They didn't get up.

So far, so good, he thought. *Now I just have to do this twenty more times or so to clear out the engineering room. Easy.*

The door to engineering slid open with a hiss. Rocka, crouched against the wall by the door, cautiously peeked around the corner. Sadly, he had been right. There were at least twenty robots in there, each with a brain on top of his or her head.

I can take out eight or ten, but not all of them, thought Rocka. *So now what?*

When he looked around the corner this time, he spent a little more time scouting. The robots were going about their jobs with precision, most likely the way they always did, despite being controlled by the brains. Rocka guessed that the brains must gain the knowledge of their hosts — that was the only way they could run a ship this complex.

If they know everything the robots knew, then they know the dangers in this place, too, he thought. *Does that mean they will react the way the robots would?*

Just inside the door, there was a catwalk. At the far end of the catwalk, thick power cables ran along the wall. Warning labels were posted all around the cables. Rocka knew enough about spaceship engineering to know that any disruption to the power flowing through those wires would be a bad thing.

He leaned in, took aim with his shield, and let it fly. It sliced through a pair of cables and buried itself in the metal wall. Rocka expected a flash of artificial lightning, a whooping alarm, and a mass evacuation from engineering.

What he got was twenty plasma blasters pointed right at him. When he turned, the two guards were back on their feet, their weapons aimed at him as well. The smiles on their faces were tight and frightening.

"I guess this is the part where I give up," said Rocka. He could hear crewbots coming up the stairs to the catwalk.

"If you're smart," said one of the guards, a brain mounted on his head.

"Doesn't look like I have any other choice," Rocka said, starting to rise.

Then, before the guards could react, Rocka dove down the staircase, slamming into the guards and knocking them back down. He somersaulted to his feet. Crewbots were rushing toward him. Rocka used his sword to knock the weapon from one, then to upend a second.

Plasma bolts flew around him, burning scorch marks into the wall. Rocka vaulted to the top of a bank of computers. As the crewbots closed in on his perch, he leapt into the midst of them.

The impact of his dive felled a handful of the crew. Rocka kicked free of the ones trying to grab him and made it to the computer console that controlled the power flow. He held his sword, point downward, above the console.

"Three guesses what happens if I plunge this

sword into this machine," Rocka said. "I'll give you a hint: It's spelled B-O-O-M and we all wind up as space junk."

"We wouldn't want that," said a voice from above. Rocka looked up to see a robot wearing the colors of a security chief. A brain was on top of his head, too.

"Then everyone puts their weapons down, now," demanded Rocka. "I'm not kidding."

"I'm sure you're not," said Kirch. "You were willing to disable this ship with your shield, after all." The security robot gestured to where the shield was still buried in the wall. "Aren't you at all curious why this trick didn't work?"

When Rocka said nothing, Kirch walked over and yanked the shield out of the wall. Then he pulled the severed wire free from its mooring and touched the exposed end to his arm. Nothing happened.

"We knew all along you would be heading here, you fool," said Kirch. "As soon as you fled auxiliary control, we rerouted everything there. The crew you saw 'hard at work' in here was putting on an act for your benefit. All the power is gone from this room."

Rocka started to say something. Then a bolt of energy shot up from the console he was hovering over, traveling up his sword and into him. He dropped like a rock to the ground, stunned.

"Well, most of the power is gone," corrected Kirch. "I guess I must have missed a little."

8

Breez was lost.

Sometime after the fight with the brain creature, she had turned right instead of left at a junction and now was moving away from the bridge instead of toward it. With no way to turn around, she had no choice but to proceed and see where she wound up.

As she crawled, she would look through each grate she passed, hoping she would spot a room that might be of use. At first, this seemed to be a waste of time, as all she was seeing was empty conference rooms. But after several minutes, she had another reason to react in surprise.

Now she was in the shafts that serviced the

ship's hangar bay. The largest single room on the *Valiant*, the bay area was used for takeoffs, landings, and storage for the ship's two shuttlecraft. It was big enough to fit a small army in, and that seemed to be exactly what it was being used for.

Lying neatly on the ground, side by side, were at least one hundred robots. None of them were moving. From a distance, Breez couldn't tell if any of them were still powered up or if they had ceased to exist. She just knew she had to get in there.

Unfortunately, there was the little problem of the electrified grate. She had nothing she could use to insulate herself against the shock and no room to throw her shield and try to open the grate that way. She would have to risk the jolt to get out of the shaft.

But before striking the blow, Breez took one more look around. That was when she noticed a very thin wire running along the top of the shaft. She reached up and touched it, feeling the unmistakable hum of power running through it. From its width and appearance, she guessed it was a low-energy communications wire, possibly linked to the ship's public address system. But all Breez cared about was that it was carrying electricity.

Carefully, she detached it from the wall and stretched it out on the floor of the shaft. Then she raised the head of her lance and let it drop, allowing the blade to slice through the wire. Breez then yanked one end of the wire free, sparks still flying from the end of it. She touched it to the grate, and there was a small electrical explosion as the barrier shorted out.

Breez punched the grate in, and it hit the floor of the hangar bay with a clang. She slipped through the opening and dropped to the ground. Immediately, she rushed to one of the silent robots.

To her relief, the crewbot was not dead. He had been powered down just enough to be in a kind of stasis.

Now things were starting to make sense. When she and Rocka had first come on board, she had noted that the sensors were not reading enough robots to run a ship this size. Maybe there weren't enough brains to control them all, so these robots had been forced into stasis somehow.

Their life signs wouldn't show up on sensors.

Breez rose and started to check on another robot when she suddenly felt dizzy. A few more steps and she almost blacked out.

Of course, she realized. *It would take too long to shut down one hundred robots one at a time. So they set up a dampening field in here that affects any robot in the room. I have to . . . find the controls . . . before . . .*

There was a flashing button on the opposite wall. That had to be the on-off switch for the field. If it wasn't, there would be no time for her to keep searching.

Aquax stood by the navigation station. Kirch had left the bridge a short time before to deal with the Hero on the engineering deck. The navigator was getting ready to start blowing the meteoroids apart.

"I can't achieve a target lock, sir, so I am going with my best guess."

"I'm sure that will be fine," said Aquax. The creature controlling the captain's body found itself strangely troubled. It wasn't sentiment or the feelings of friendship the real Aquax had for Stormer that were bothering the brain. The creatures absorbed knowledge, not emotion, from their hosts.

No, what was bothering Aquax was the waste of resources. The swarm leader was determined to destroy Stormer. But if Stormer could be taken over, imagine the knowledge the swarm would gain! Every last secret of Hero Factory had to be known to the Alpha Team leader. Its destruction would be simplicity itself once those secrets were revealed, and Stormer himself could lead the final attack.

"Hold your fire," Aquax said abruptly.

"But, sir, the swarm leader—"

"—Isn't here right now," Aquax finished for him. "I am in command. If Stormer reappears on your sensors, I want you to open Airlock Four. Do you understand?"

"Yes, sir," the navigator said, making a mental

note to let Kirch know about this at the earliest opportunity. This was treason, after all.

The creature controlling Aquax knew how his actions must look. But he would be vindicated once the most famous Hero of all was just one more slave of the swarm.

Forcing herself to keep moving, Breez stumbled across the room, trying not to step on or trip over any of the robots.

Just as consciousness was about to leave her, she hit the button with her hand. Within thirty seconds, Breez started to feel better. A few minutes later, the robots began to stir.

One of the robots, a repair tech, was the first to notice Breez. "Hey, I recognize you!"

"You do?" said Breez, genuinely surprised.

"Sure, I saw you on the news vids when all those crooks broke out of jail," said the tech. "You're Wind . . . Gust . . . um . . ."

"Breez," she offered gently. "Are you all right?"

The tech looked around at his colleagues, all getting to their feet. "Yeah, everyone seems to be okay. Do you know what's going on? Captain Aquax ordered us all to report here, and the next thing we knew we were losing consciousness, and then . . . well, here you are."

"I don't know the whole picture yet," said Breez. "But this ship is under hostile control. The bridge will know you're all awake in a matter of moments, if they don't already. Security will be headed down here to try and put you back to sleep again."

"We won't let them," said one robot.

"Let them try!" said another.

"Listen to me," said Breez. "You have to get out of here. Get to the armory and grab weapons. We'll try to retake the bridge. Now, who here can pilot a shuttlecraft?"

About twenty hands went up. Breez pointed to two of them. "Get in those ships and head for Hero Factory. Tell them the *Valiant* has been hijacked by aliens who have taken control of the crew. Rocka and I are trying to recapture control. Got that?"

The two crewbots nodded and bolted for the ships. Meanwhile, Breez led the other robots out of the hangar. She turned back to look through the circular window in the door and watch the shuttlecraft take off. The hangar doors opened to allow the vehicles to depart. But to Breez's amazement, before the craft could fly out, something else flew in!

"Stormer!" she shouted as her team leader collapsed on the deck.

The two shuttlecraft launched, heading for Hero Factory. Breez immediately shut the hangar doors behind them and then rushed out to see to the new arrival.

"Stormer, what are you doing here? Are you injured?"

The Alpha Team leader shook his head. "Just . . . exhausted. Flew a long way . . . had to find out . . ."

"Things are about as bad as they can be," she

said, quickly relating to him everything she had learned. "The crew is arming themselves. I don't know what's happened to Rocka, but I can't wait for him. This ship has to be stopped."

"You're right. We're running out of time," said Stormer. "I left orders to blow this ship out of the sky if it doesn't change course."

Breez's response was cut off by the sound of the door from the corridor opening. She thought it might be some of the crew coming back for her. Instead, she turned to see an impressive-looking robot with a brain on its head and two more brains crawling along beside him. The robot carried a plasma weapon, which was pointed at Breez and Stormer.

"Stand very still," said the newcomer. "I do not want to have to hurt you."

"Aquax . . . ?" Stormer said, momentarily surprised. Then his eyes fixed on the brain that controlled his friend, and his voice turned ice-cold. "Let my friend go. Whatever you were planning, it's over."

The brain made Aquax chuckle. "It hasn't

even begun, Stormer. It won't begin until Hero Factory is eliminated as a potential threat. And you are going to help make that happen."

Aquax gestured to the two brains. "There's one for each of you. Once they are in place, they will know everything you know."

"Never," said Stormer. It wasn't yelled in defiance or hurled like a threat. It was a simple statement of fact.

"It's not so bad, really," Aquax continued. "What does your independent thought get you? Worry and heartache and dealing with all the consequences of bad decisions . . . once we are in control, that all goes away."

"Along with everything that makes us ourselves," said Breez. "Justify it however you like, you're still parasites . . . monsters."

"But we are monsters that are winning," Aquax replied. "Isn't that what counts?"

The two brains rapidly crawled across the room toward Stormer and Breez.

"It's not painful, I assure you," Aquax said. "After a moment, you just . . . fade away. Your mind isn't gone; it's just no longer needed."

"Sorry, I still have use for mine," growled Stormer. "I need to think up an appropriate way to make you pay for all this."

Aquax shook his head in mock sadness. "No, you see, you really have no choice in the matter. You can become one with us . . . or you can cease to exist."

Evo's sensor scope suddenly lit up. Two vessels were heading for the hastily improvised fleet of Hero craft. After a few moments, the ship's computer identified them as shuttlecraft from the *Valiant*.

They must have spotted us, he thought. *They're sending out the shuttles to slow us down.*

He activated his communicator. "This is Evo to all Hero craft. We have to assume any craft coming from the *Valiant* is potentially hostile. Prepare to engage those shuttlecraft. Disable them if possible, but stop them however you can."

The half dozen Hero craft banked to the right as one and prepared to attack the two shuttlecraft.

"You know this isn't going to work, right?" asked Rocka. Two of the controlled crewbots had pinned his arms, holding him so he couldn't get away.

"It seems to be working fine so far," said the Kirch creature.

"Do you know how many would-be galactic conquerors Hero Factory deals with every week? It's what we *do*."

Kirch smiled. "You have never dealt with anything like us."

"Wow, haven't heard that one before," said Rocka. "If you're waiting for me to beg for mercy, you'll be waiting a long time."

The wall speaker crackled. "Bridge to swarm leader."

Kirch hit the "Send" button. "I am here."

"The uncontrolled crewbots have escaped the hangar bay, and both shuttlecraft have launched," reported the navigator. "And . . . Stormer is on board."

"Where is he?"

"Hangar bay, sir."

"Patch me through. It seems we may have use for this stray Hero we found after all."

The voice of Kirch boomed through the hangar. "Stormer. I have one of your Heroes. I suggest you surrender."

"I'm a little busy right now," Stormer replied. "I'm about to get brain-attacked, or so someone thinks."

Kirch didn't have to think hard to guess whom Stormer was talking about. "Aquax, you will cease. I will decide when these Heroes join the swarm, not you."

"No!" snapped Aquax. "I am doing what is best for our mission!"

The brains crept closer, ready to spring on Stormer and Breez. Just as they pushed off the ground, twin plasma bolts hit the creatures, knocking them senseless. Aquax turned around, only to get hit by a bolt and also rendered unconscious.

Standing in the doorway was Xera, plasma weapon in hand. "It looked like something needed to be done."

"Thank you," said Breez.

Stormer rushed to Aquax's side and was trying to pry the brain off his head.

"Be careful," said Xera. "Do it the wrong way and you could damage your friend. He needs medical care."

"What's going on in there?" demanded Kirch. "Aquax, report!"

Stormer looked up at the speaker mounted on the wall. "Now, you listen to me, you miserable, bodiless pile of tissue. I'm coming for you. Hero

Factory is coming for you. And when we're done with you, we'll find wherever you came from and lock it up so tight a microbe couldn't escape."

"I have the ship," Kirch replied. "I have your friend. Hero Factory has less than thirty minutes to exist."

"But you don't have us," said Stormer. "And a lot can happen in a short time."

With that, Stormer aimed his plasma blaster and fired at the wall speaker, blowing it to pieces.

"Let's go," said Stormer. "Rocka would look stupid with one of those things on his head."

9

Furno knocked on the door of Bulk's quarters. "I have a message from Evo."

The door slid open. Bulk looked awful, as if he had let his energy level slip down way too low.

"You need a recharge," said Furno. "We can't afford to have you go down right now."

"I'll get to it," said Bulk. "What did you hear?"

"They're in battle with a couple of *Valiant* shuttlecraft. Evo figures it's a delaying action. At the rate the ship is moving, it will be on top of them any minute now."

Bulk turned around and walked away from Furno. "A lot of good robots are going to go down today. If only there was some way to shove that ship back where it came from. . . ."

"Shove . . . ?" repeated Furno. "Wait a second, maybe you've got something."

Furno hit the wall communicator. "Furno to Evo — do you read?"

"I'm kind of busy right now!" came the response.

"What's the situation?" asked Bulk.

"They're claiming not to be enemies," Evo replied. "They have some crazy story about alien brains taking over their crew. They say Breez sent them to warn us."

"Maybe she did," said Bulk. "Break off the attack. Let them pass. Whatever they're up to, we can handle it on this end. I think Furno has something he needs you to do."

"Evo, listen carefully," said Furno. "Each Hero craft has a tractor beam for holding things in place or drawing them toward you. I think we can use that to stop the *Valiant*."

"Furno, none of these ships has a beam powerful enough to stop a ship that size."

"Not alone, no," Furno countered. "But if you reverse the beams and combine them into one, then hit the *Valiant* head-on with it—"

"I got it," Evo replied. "Maybe we can hold them in place, or even push them back a little."

"And if they keep trying to go forward?" asked Bulk.

"Maybe they burn out their engines," said Furno. "If nothing else, we might buy a few minutes to think of something else. It's worth a try."

"Do it," ordered Bulk. "Grab that ship and ram it past the edge of the galaxy if you have to."

"Yes, sir," said Evo. "Over and out."

"Come on," said Bulk. "We have a message to send."

The two Heroes walked out of Bulk's quarters and down the corridor.

"To whom?" asked Furno. "Stormer's out of range by now."

"Who said anything about Stormer? Or even using the radio? We've got one more Hero craft; it just got out of the repair dock. You and I are taking it."

"Going where?"

Bulk smiled. "Kid, Evo is going to bring that ship to a standstill, and then we're going to knock on their door . . . hard."

"What are you going to do?" asked Xera as he, Stormer, and Breez ran through the corridors of the *Valiant*. "There are so many of them, and they're so powerful."

"From what Breez tells me, a hundred crewbots are going to start cutting their numbers down," Stormer answered. "As for power, they are only as powerful as the bodies they control. We'll do what we have to do to eliminate those bodies as a threat."

Breez wanted to ask just what Stormer meant. He surely wasn't talking about harming the crew, who were innocent victims in all this . . . was he? But she did not want to question his plans in front of Xera, who was frightened and unstable enough already.

So instead, she asked, "Where are we going? Engineering is three decks below. That's where Rocka must be."

"We're headed to auxiliary control," answered Stormer. "We're taking back control of this ship."

"But—"

"Think, Breez. What's Rocka best at, besides putting things together?"

That was an easy question. "Taking them apart," she answered.

"Exactly. This ship is running just fine. But you and I both know Rocka would have fought his way through the engine room and broken *something* before he was captured. So why didn't he?"

The pieces fell into place in Breez's mind. "Because there was nothing to break. They transferred power to auxiliary before he ever got there so he wouldn't do any damage."

"Right. So we go there, and whoever is in our way . . . won't be for long. Once we have the ship off this collision course, Hero Factory can deal with the brains."

There was a flash of light. Stormer cried out as a plasma bolt struck him from behind, knocking him to the ground. Breez whirled to see Xera, his weapon aimed at her.

"I'm afraid I can't let you do that," said the science officer.

"Are you crazy?!" exclaimed Breez. "We're trying to help you!"

"You're trying to stop the brains, and you mustn't. They're right. Trying to think for ourselves has caused all the problems in this universe. If we just let them think for us—"

"You're a traitor," Breez said, her voice like a steel whip. "You let those monsters on board, didn't you?"

"No," replied Xera, shaking his head. "It happened just like I said. Kirch let the brain loose and it took him over. He let the rest of the swarm into the ship. They were going to control me, too, but I . . . talked them out of it."

"How?" Breez asked. She had to keep him talking to give Stormer time to recover.

"I told them they were going to need a representative to the rest of the galaxy, someone who wouldn't frighten everyone. I could speak for them. I could prepare everyone for their coming. Maybe I could make others understand that theirs is a better way."

"Brains controlling our bodies is a better way? How can you even think that?"

Xera laughed harshly. "Look what Hero Factory just went through, Breez. Criminal robots escaping from prison, causing all sorts of damage before you recaptured them. Were they made bad? No. Something went wrong with their thinking and they *became* bad.

"With the brains in control," Xera continued, "that can never happen again. There won't be any need for villains . . . or Heroes. Everyone will do what is needed for the good of the swarm."

"And what if some of us don't want to live that way?" asked Breez.

"Then you would be a threat, and you would be . . . dealt with."

"Xera, you helped me before. . . ."

"No, I didn't. I let you get into the shafts because I thought it would be faster and easier for you to be brained in there. But you were too resourceful. You freed the crew before I could get there to stop you."

"And Aquax?"

"He disobeyed the orders of the swarm leader. He had to be punished."

Okay, I can't wait for Stormer anymore, Breez said to herself. *This robot has blown a circuit. Time to take him down.*

"I know what you're doing," said Xera. "You're hoping Stormer will wake up and rescue you. I'll make sure he'll never wake up again!"

"You've got it all wrong, Xera," said Breez.

Faster than his eye could follow, she lashed out with her lance, knocking him off his feet. Before he could move, she had the sharp point against his throat.

"I'm a Hero. I rescue myself."

Rocka was calculating the odds.

Word had come down that Stormer and Breez were headed away from engineering, most likely going to auxiliary control. Kirch had sent ten of his crew there to stop them. That left ten here to keep an eye on Rocka.

Ten is good, he thought. *I can do ten.*

Stormer wasn't stopping, which meant Rocka would be expendable in Kirch's eyes. But before he did anything to the Hero, he would need to transfer power back to engineering to make sure he stayed in command of the ship. It was going to be up to Rocka to prevent that.

He had an advantage. They had taken his sword and shield, but the weapons had been designed to respond to a particular transmission frequency. All Rocka had to do was activate it using the cybernetics in his helmet.

The signal was sent. He could see the sword and shield stirring on the table on which they rested, almost as if they were waking up. Rocka waited for the moment when most of the crew was occupied with the preparation of the power transfer. Then he summoned his weapons.

The shield flew through the air, impacting one of the two robots who held Rocka. At the same time, the sword landed in Rocka's hand. He used the hilt to bash the other guard. Now he was free.

"Stop him!" Kirch ordered.

But there was no stopping Rocka now. He was everywhere at once, hitting and running, moving too fast for the crewbots to take aim with their weapons. He knew he might not win the battle, but he needed to buy Stormer time.

As the brain-controlled crew fell all around him, Rocka allowed himself to hope. If he could retake engineering, the crisis would be over. He moved faster, taking on two and three opponents at once. Felling the last of the crew, he felt a surge of satisfaction.

That lasted until he felt a plasma weapon in his back. He had forgotten about Kirch.

"Very . . . acrobatic," the swarm leader said. "But futile. This ship is ours. Hero Factory will not take it from us . . . but we will deliver it to them, with fire and thunder."

"For brains with no mouths, you guys sure talk a lot," Rocka shot back. "We don't make speeches at Hero Factory. We just take action."

"You're right. It is time for action," said Kirch, his finger tightening on the trigger of his weapon. "Good-bye, Hero."

The ship suddenly lurched violently. Kirch lost his balance, his shot going wild. Before Rocka could take advantage of the opening, the ship rocked again and the Hero found himself on the floor. Kirch got back to his feet and ran for the exit.

Evo's voice suddenly rang through the loud-speakers. "Attention, *Valiant*. This is Evo, representing Hero Factory. You have been halted in space. You will power down your engines and surrender."

Rocka jumped up and let out a whoop of celebration. Kirch might still be on the run, but

Hero Factory was on the job. *This adventure is almost over*, Rocka thought to himself.

He couldn't imagine how wrong he was.

Kirch made it to the bridge. "Full power to weapons!" he shouted as he entered. "Clear those Hero craft from our path!"

"Yes, sir."

Kirch smiled. He could see the six Hero craft on the screen, pushing the *Valiant* back with tractor beams. It had to be taking all the power those smaller ships possessed to hold a vessel this size at bay. They would have no power left for weapons or shields. His ship would blow them to atoms.

That would be the first sign that the fall of Hero Factory had begun.

10

Stormer and Breez were fighting for their lives.

Just as they had reached the corridor that led to auxiliary control, ten crewbots had appeared, all of them armed and dangerous. They were joined by brains that had been inside the control room, springing from wall to wall, trying to affix themselves to Stormer's and Breez's heads.

Stormer crouched around a corner, using his plasma weapon to knock the blasters out of the crewbots' hands. Breez, on the other hand, charged into the melee, using her lance and her moves to take down enemy fighters.

"Breez, find cover!" Stormer yelled. "There are too many of them!"

Breez planted one end of her lance in the floor and swung around it, landing a kick in the midsection of an attacker. In one smooth motion, she used the lance to take out two more.

"Not anymore, there aren't," she shouted back.

Stormer had to admit that Breez's combat skills were amazing. But she still hadn't mastered watching her back. A plasma bolt from his weapon took out a crewbot about to grab her from behind. Spotting a half-dozen brains getting ready to spring, Stormer leapt from cover and used his power sword to bat them away, shocking them into unconsciousness in the process.

When the last of the defenders had fallen, Breez surveyed the scene. "Not bad," she said.

"Stop trying to impress me," Stormer said as he walked into auxiliary control.

"What do you—?"

"There were easier ways to stop that mob," Stormer continued. "Ways that wouldn't put you at risk. But you just waded into the fight like

Bulk, without thinking about strategy."

Breez felt herself growing angry. "It worked, didn't it?"

Stormer wheeled on her. "That's not the point. I know you can fight hard, Breez . . . but if you want to last as a Hero, you have to fight smart."

Breez didn't say anything. Stormer softened his tone a little and said, "You're a valuable asset to Hero Factory. I simply don't want to lose you. Like I said, you don't have to try to impress me — I'm already impressed."

She brightened immediately. "You are?"

Stormer, however, had now turned his attention to the controls. He was amazed that the brains hadn't transferred power out of here and back to engineering. Somehow, he had a feeling he had Rocka to thank for that.

A closer look at the consoles, though, filled him with worry. Those concerns were heightened when the ship shuddered again, this time with the distinctive feel of weapons fire. The *Valiant* was attacking the Hero craft!

Desperately, Stormer tried to stop the battle,

but weapons control was locked onto the bridge. "Breez, you're going to have to head for the command center and stop that attack. Otherwise, our ships don't stand a chance."

"Right," Breez said, before running off down the corridor.

Now it was up to Stormer. Navigation and speed could still be controlled from down here, but he would have to work fast. Once the brains realized he had made it to auxiliary control, they would cut it off and all the equipment would be useless.

He got to work, but his mind was on Evo and the other Heroes. If Breez couldn't seize the bridge, any Hero craft nearby would be doomed. They were going to need a miracle to get out of this one intact.

Kirch could feel the tide turning. The *Valiant* had already disabled two of the Hero craft, and the rest would not last for long. With the tractor beam power reduced by almost half, it was only a matter of time before his ship could move forward again and sweep the enemy out of the sky.

He was about to give the command to obliterate the remaining ships when the *Valiant* rocked violently to port as the bridge lights flicked on and off.

"We've been hit on the starboard side, sir," reported the navigator. "There's another Hero craft!"

"Hard to starboard," Kirch growled. "We'll give them a welcome."

"Yes, sir, I — sir! We've lost the helm! Navigation controls won't respond."

Stormer, thought Kirch darkly.

"Auxiliary control has been taken," he said. "Send every available crewbot there to take it back. Now!"

"Communications are down, too, sir."

"Then go tell them personally!" Kirch shouted.

The navigator jumped up from his chair and headed for the elevator. The door slid open to reveal Bulk and Furno.

"Hi, fellas," said Bulk. "You took something that didn't belong to you . . . in fact, a lot of somethings. We're here to get it all back."

The bridge crew got to their feet, ready to fight. Kirch waved them back. Oddly, he didn't seem at all disturbed by the discovery that two more Heroes were on his ship.

"Very well," he said. "Get Stormer up here. It is time you realized just what you are up against."

Stormer and Breez had joined Bulk and Furno on the bridge. Rocka was in auxiliary control, making sure it stayed in Hero Factory hands. The *Valiant* had been brought to a stop, but most of the brain-controlled crew was still loose on the ship.

Kirch was sitting in the command chair, looking like he was still in complete control of the situation. Stormer found that annoying. Breez was worried that the brain might have one more trick to play.

"Time to end this," said Stormer. "I don't know why you were targeting Hero Factory, but the *Valiant* won't be heading there today. Let your host bodies go and give up."

"Let them go," Kirch said, drumming his fingers on the arm of the chair. "Yes, we could do that. But . . . if we don't do it the right way . . . none of them will survive the separation."

"Then do it the right way," Stormer said icily.

Kirch stood up. "Get off my ship. Do it now, or every one of us will doom our host bodies."

"If we leave, you hit Hero Factory," said Bulk, "and everybody in the crew is toast, anyhow."

"No, they won't, and they know it," said Stormer. "I spoke to Evo. Hero Factory has summoned reserves from the local systems. There's a fleet waiting for the *Valiant*. You can't win, brain, no matter what you do."

"Perhaps not," agreed Kirch. "But you can lose."

"What are your terms?" asked Stormer.

"You leave the ship, with any noncontrolled robots you wish. You can even take Xera. We will keep the *Valiant* and pilot it away from here. You will guarantee no pursuit."

Stormer smiled bitterly and shook his head. "I have a better idea." He spoke into his helmet microphone. "Rocka, go ahead."

The ship shuddered as it suddenly took on a new course. Kirch glanced at the viewscreen, only to see it dominated by a fiery ball of gas.

"That's the sun in this system, and we're flying right toward it," said Stormer. "In a few minutes, we'll all be cinders. You won't get the *Valiant*, you won't get Hero Factory . . . you *will* get roasted, and all for nothing. Or you can give up now. Your choice."

Kirch looked from the screen to Stormer and back to the screen again. "You're bluffing. It would mean the destruction of your team."

The elevator door opened. Captain Aquax walked in, brain still atop his head. "He's not bluffing. Every member of Hero Factory is prepared to give their life for justice . . . Aquax knows that about them, so I do, too."

Kirch thought for a long time. Then he said,

"All right. I will order all the members of my species to assemble in the hangar bay along with their hosts. We will do the separation then."

A very short time later, the four Heroes and dozens of controlled robots were assembled in the massive hangar bay. Also present were the brains that did not have hosts.

"This is not the end, you know," said Kirch.

"It's close enough," said Stormer. "I'll take it."

Kirch nodded. "We are prepared to separate. You can change course now."

Stormer shook his head. "We'll stay on course, for now. But we will slow down to give you time to do what you need to do."

Switching to his helmet mike, Stormer said, "Rocka, decrease our speed."

There was a long pause. Then Rocka broadcast back, "I'm trying, Stormer. Something's wrong. We're not slowing down!"

"Try a manual override," ordered Stormer.

"It's no good. Speed is actually increasing!"

"Change course, now, get us away from that sun!"

"I can't do that, either!"

Stormer looked at Kirch. "What did you do?"

"I hoped for victory, but prepared for defeat," Kirch replied. "I had a safeguard installed. No one has control of this ship now, Stormer. The *Valiant* is going to burn."

Before anyone could react, Kirch rushed to the wall and hit the control that opened the hangar bay doors.

"Good-bye, Stormer. I am sure we will meet again."

Suddenly, the brains detached from the heads of their hosts. The robots collapsed to the ground. The brains leapt and crawled toward the opening doors and outer space.

"We have to go after them," yelled Furno.

"No time," said Stormer. "The air is going to be sucked out of here in a few seconds. We have to get the crew out of this room."

Even as he said it, Stormer knew it was

impossible. Four Heroes could not carry this many robots to safety in so short a time.

It was then that the door from the corridor burst open. The robots Breez had rescued poured in, grabbing their shipmates and dragging them to safety. Working with the Heroes, they were able to get everyone out in time.

Just before leaving the hangar, Stormer looked back. The brains had made it out of the doors and into space. They had only forgotten one thing—thanks to Kirch's tampering, the speeding *Valiant* was practically right on top of a sun. No sooner had they escaped the confines of the vessel than they were turned into puffs of ash by the intense heat.

"Or maybe I won't meet you again," muttered Stormer.

"We're going to be joining them pretty soon if we don't find a way to stop this ship," said Bulk.

"Furno, go help Rocka. Breez, Bulk, with me—we're heading for engineering. The rest of you, get back to your posts."

"If you don't mind, I'm coming with you,"

said Aquax, now free of the brain that had been controlling him.

"It's your ship, Captain," Stormer replied.

Furno held a scanner over the main engineering control unit. "We can't turn the ship, and we can't slow it down," he reported.

"Never mind what we can't do," said Stormer. "What *can* we do?"

"There is one thing," said Aquax. "But it's beyond dangerous. I doubt we'd survive it."

"Well, I know we won't survive that sun," said Bulk. "So spill it, Captain."

"We can shut the engines down completely," Aquax said. "Just cut them off."

"The stress would tear the ship apart," said Furno. "Plus, the gravity of the sun would still draw us in."

"And with that galedanium on board, this ship will go up in an explosion big enough to be seen in half the galaxy."

"Galedanium?" asked Breez. "Maybe . . . maybe that's the answer."

"What do you have in mind, Breez?" asked Stormer.

"If we eject the galedanium out in front of the ship, it will explode and might send us hurtling back away from the sun."

"Torn apart *and* blown up," said Bulk. "What a great plan."

"It's all we've got," said Stormer. "Aquax, get to the bridge. Furno, help Breez with the galedanium. Bulk and I will take care of the engines."

"See you guys soon," said Bulk. "Either in here, or floating around out there."

Everything was ready. Rocka had warned the Hero craft away. Bulk and Stormer were ready to cut off the engines. Furno and Breez had the explosives ready to be launched. Time was running out — if the ship didn't hit the sun, the sheer heat would set off the galedanium.

"Better do it now," Aquax radioed down from the bridge. "We're closing in on the sun."

"Right," said Stormer. "Shutting down now. Breez, get ready for launch."

Stormer hit the button that would shut down the engines. Immediately, a digital countdown started, indicating they had three minutes until the engines went offline.

"Aquax, this says we have three minutes to full stop," said Stormer. "We don't have three minutes left!"

"It's the engines," said Aquax. "They've been running at high speed for so long, it's going to take time to cut them off."

"Nah, it won't," said Bulk. He walked up to the main engine and started punching holes in it.

"Bulk, what are you — ?"

"Hey, what's the worst that happens?" said Bulk. "We blow up sixty seconds sooner?"

It felt like the ship suddenly came to a wrenching stop, with everyone being hurled forward by the abrupt change in velocity. When Bulk regained his feet, he said, "See? When in doubt, hit something."

"Breez, now!" Stormer barked into his helmet mike.

Furno and Breez shoved the explosive into the airlock. Once the last door was opened, the crates were drawn out into space.

"Get down!" yelled Furno.

The explosives drifted away from the ship, floating slowly through space. Then the rays of the sun struck them, heating up their unstable cargo. The next instant, there was a massive explosion.

For the *Valiant*, it was like slamming into a concrete wall in space at light speed. The ship flew backward, tumbling end over end, thousands of tons of metal tossed like a leaf in a strong wind. Wave after wave of explosive energy struck the vessel, cracking the hull, shattering the external weapons systems, turning the communications array to dust.

Was it minutes, hours, or days before the ship

stopped its wild flight? No one on board could say. Battered and worn as the ship now was, the robots dragged themselves to their feet, checking to see if both they and their surroundings were intact.

Outside, the three remaining Hero craft that were still functioning flew in to begin a rescue mission. In a matter of hours, they would be joined by more ships from Hero Factory, as well as vessels from the frontier worlds. Everyone would be evacuated to Hero Factory for repair work and rest.

As for the *Valiant*, it was badly damaged. Repair crews estimated at least eighteen months before it could fly again. Mr. Makuro personally assured Captain Aquax that Hero Factory would station Heroes on the frontier to protect those worlds, no matter the cost.

Finally, there came the day the crewbots had to leave for their own worlds. Stormer and Aquax met for a final good-bye.

"That went well," Aquax said dryly. "I guess

we're even now. You got in over your head once . . . and I got something on top of mine."

"You could always join Hero Factory," said Stormer. "My pilots could use training from an expert."

"No, I'm too much my own robot," Aquax replied. "I need to be out there, running my own ship."

"You will be," Stormer assured him.

"Stormer, thank you . . . to you and to your team," said Aquax. "And do us all a favor . . . find what did this. Find it and stop it."

Stormer nodded. As his friend left, he realized that neither one of them really thought this was over.

Epilogue

Stormer sat in his office, recording a report on the events aboard the *Valiant*. A datapad sat on a corner of his desk. The text it displayed was Bulk's letter of resignation.

The buzzer sounded. "Come in," said Stormer.

Bulk entered. His eyes darted to the datapad as he tried to get an idea of whether Stormer had read it or not. Then he stood at attention, or the closest that Bulk ever came to it.

"You wanted to see me?" said Bulk.

"That's right," said Stormer, not looking up at him. The Alpha Team leader reached out, picked up the datapad, and held it toward Bulk. "Resignation not accepted."

"Now, wait—"

"Yes, you disobeyed orders, but you did it for a good reason. You judged, correctly, that I was letting my friendship for Captain Aquax interfere with my decision making. If it had not been for that, I might have made the same decision you did."

"I hope I never have to make that kind of a decision again," said Bulk.

"You did it when you had to, because you're a Hero," said Stormer, looking up at his old friend. "So I am returning your resignation datapad and not informing Mr. Makuro of your offer to quit. You're needed here. Besides, you're not going to leave me to deal with all these rookies on my own."

Bulk smiled, but the expression did not last for long. "What about the brains, or whatever they were? Think that was the end of them?"

Stormer gave Bulk a skeptical look. "No, and neither do you. We'll see them again. Probably sooner than we'd like."

"What makes you think so?"

"The *Valiant* incident felt like they saw an opportunity and seized it. I don't think it was part of a plan," Stormer replied. "I think the real plan is still to be executed."

"Executed?" Bulk said, wincing a little. "I wish you'd picked a better word."

Stormer leaned back in his chair, a grim expression on his face. "We don't know what they are, or where they came from. We do know they were willing to crash that ship into Hero Factory . . . so they're okay with dying to achieve their ends. I think we're up against a dangerous foe, Bulk."

"Yeah," Bulk chuckled. "Makes you miss the days we went up against harmless foes, doesn't it?"

Stormer managed a small smile. "All right, I get your point. If you have so much time on your hands that you can write resignation datapads, it seems like you need a new mission. So let's talk about what that's going to be. . . ."

In the training room, Breez easily swatted away the last of the rammers. Watching from the control center, Rocka nodded approvingly and shut down the program.

"Your reaction time is up," he said. "You beat the program 0.3 seconds faster than last time."

Breez nodded but said nothing. She had seemed distracted since returning from the *Valiant*.

"What's the matter? We won, didn't we?"

"Xera fooled me," she answered. "I'm Hero Factory; I can't afford to be tricked like that."

"And he ended up flat on his back, thanks to you," Rocka reminded her. "Listen, we both went on that mission feeling like we were unappreciated here. I think it's safe to say that's changed. Anyone who doubted we have what it takes isn't doubting anymore—and that includes us, right?"

Breez gave a small smile. "Right. Hey, what

do you think our next mission will be?"

Now it was Rocka's turn to be serious. "I have a funny feeling we won't be going out on our next mission. I think it will be coming to us."

"What do you mean?"

"Those brains have it in for Hero Factory. They're not going to quit 'cause we beat them once. They'll be back."

Breez nodded. "Then maybe you better turn those rammers on again. I want to be ready."

Rocka did as he was asked, saying under his breath, "But can you ever be ready for . . . the brains?"

The adventure continues in

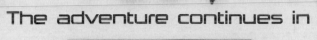

SECRET MISSION #4:
ROBOT RAMPAGE

As soon as Stringer sends a warning message from the peaceful vacation planet Tranquis VII, he vanishes.

Stormer quickly dispatches Bulk and Furno to find out what has happened to their teammate and seek out whatever threat has made the entire planet go radio silent.

Once again, the brains have taken over almost all intelligent life on the planet. But things are different this time around. Bulk and Furno are about to discover that what looks like another invasion attempt is just covering up a much deeper and more sinister plot that will rock Hero Factory to its core.